PUPPY PACK ADVEN

GW00870188

Dan Colegate, Esther Dingley & Kim Prior

Copyright © 2020 Dan Colegate. All rights reserved.

Thank you for purchasing this book.

This book or any portion thereof may not be reproduced or used in any manner whatsoever without the express written permission of the publisher except for the use of brief quotations in a book review.

www.estheranddan.com

STORIES IN THIS BOOK:

Bounding Bella Spreads A Smile

Bounding Bella was up at dawn,
ready to chase and have some fun.
Even though the sun was barely up
she felt the luckiest of pups.

To be awake on such a day,
the perfect day to explore and play
and see what treasures lay ahead,
it was better to be up than stay in bed!

So she crept into the human's room,

where they still slept within the gloom,

but Bella knew how to change that quick

by giving their tickly toes a lick.

"Oh Bella, not again" they said

as they sat up and rubbed their head,

before reaching down to pat her snout,

"I suppose you're ready to go out?"

So with Bella smiling by the door,

her tail thumping on the floor,

the human slipped into their clothes

and said to Bella, "where should we go?"

Together they bounded to the park,

the sky was bright, no longer dark,

with feathery birds singing in the trees

and the warm air filled with busy bees.

"Oh what a wondrous place to be
for a bounding pup as lucky as me!"
thought Bella as she charged around
and raced across the dew-soaked ground.

Her human threw some balls and sticks,
which Bella fetched and did some tricks,
then chased the shadows of butterflies.
She never caught one, but she always tried.

"I wish that everyone could be

as happy and full of joy as me"

thought Bella as she stopped by the lake

and sat down to take a little break.

That's when she spotted, on a bench nearby,

a lone old man who was starting to cry,

with his head held tight within his hands

and his tears falling on the lakeside sand

"Oh my" thought Bella, "that's awfully bad,

to be alone and to be so sad,

I wonder if I can share my smile

and cheer him up for a little while?"

So moving closer to the man,

she ran tight circles in the sand,

to show him how happy life could look

with simple play, that's all it took.

But no matter how hard Bella tried,

she just couldn't catch the old man's eye,

as he continued to sit and weep

from his lonely lakeside seat.

So when the circles didn't work

Bella tried turning somersaults,

leaping so far into the sky

it almost looked like she could fly.

Yet still the man didn't look at all,

not even when Bella dug a hole

so deep and wide that she disappeared,

all except the tops of her ears.

Baffled Bella eventually stood,

her digging and jumping had done no good,

but what else could she possibly do

to stop the man feeling quite so blue?

That's when she had a new idea,

the answer was suddenly so clear,

maybe he just needed a friend

to sit and help the crying end.

So edging closer to the seat,

Bella sat quietly by his feet

until moments later a hand reached out

and rested softly on her snout.

Wiping away a final tear,
"It's so lovely that you're here"
said the man as he smiled down,
washing away his previous frown.

"I was just so lonely, that was why
I couldn't help but sit and cry.
But your kind gesture has reminded me
how friendly even strangers can be".

That's when Bella began to hear

her human's shouting getting near.

"Bella. Bella! Where are you now?

"It's breakfast time. We have to go".

Bella Bella breakfast

Moments later Bella could see

her human coming through the trees,

calling across to the man in blue,

"I'm sorry, is she bothering you?"

"Quite the opposite" she heard the old man say.

"This little pup has made my day".

THE END

Awesome George Saves The Day

Awesome George wanted to play

while all his sisters slept one day,

so he tried to pass the time alone

by chewing on his soft toy bone.

"This bone tastes good, but it's not as fun

as going outside to chase and run",

thought George as he sat and looked around,

when all of a sudden he heard a sound.

A banging, clanging, scary knocking,

which to other pups might have been quite shocking,

but brave young George saw it was nothing more

than the wind blowing open the kitchen door.

Well, George was never one to miss

a chance to have some fun like this,

so leaving his snoozing sisters behind

he stretched his legs and strolled outside.

And the first thing that he noticed there

was the human in her garden chair,

dozing and dreaming and snoring so loud

she was noisier than a football crowd!

which is probably why she couldn't hear,

as Awesome George sneaked ever so near,

through their chair legs and continued past

into the long, long garden grass.

"Well, this is a grand adventure for sure"

thought Awesome George as he explored,

leaving the house far, far behind

to see what games and fun he'd find.

First he found a lot of sticks,

which he quickly chewed into smaller bits,

and then he surprised a wriggling worm

that was digging near an old milk churn.

For a while he chased a butterfly,

but eventually it got too high,

so instead he decided he would dig

an enormous hole, both deep and big.

But just as he was about to start

to push the grass and soil apart,

he heard a frightened, small voice cry,

"I've hurt my wing and cannot fly".

And George, not sure if he'd really heard,

looked up to see a baby bird

flapping on a nearby mound,

unable to get up off the ground.

"Don't be afraid, I'll be there quick"

called George to the young, frightened chick,

and with that he began to bound

to join the bird upon the mound.

"What happened here, what can I do?"

said George to the little scared cuckoo.

"Well, I fell out of the nest you see,

and banged my wing upon this tree".

"And now, until my mum gets home

I have to wait here all alone

and I'm really scared, as scared as can be

that the cat is going to come after me".

"I'm Awesome George, I have no fear,

I'll make sure there's no cat near here".

And with that George set right about

keeping watch and looking out.

And hiding quietly behind the tree,

sure enough, he could soon see

a cat's tail flicking up nearby,

so barking out a warning cry

He charged across the grassy floor

towards the tail, barking more,

he scared the hungry cat away.

It wouldn't scare the chick that day!

A while later they heard the sound

of bigger wings flapping to the ground.

"Oh there you are" said the chick's scared mum

"all alone in the hot, hot sun".

"Well, actually I'm safe you see,

because Awesome George looked after me".

"Oh, thank you George" exclaimed the mum,

"without you that cat would've surely come".

And George's chest swelled up with pride,

he felt so brave and strong inside.

"Time to head home and tell the pack,

they'll be excited to see me when I'm back".

"Oh George where have you ever been?"

said his sisters as he crept back in.

"Up to no good I bet" said one,

"he's always in trouble when he's gone".

And so George decided not to say

just how brave he'd been that day,

because it didn't matter if his sister knew,

so he settled down for a quiet chew.

THE END

Poorly Pati

And The

Friendly Ghost

"Why do I have to stay behind,

when all the others go outside?"

moaned Pati as the door swung closed,

and almost banged her sniffly nose.

"Oh, being poorly is just no fun,

I want to go out and chase and run.

But just because I have a cold

I have to stay in like I'm told".

Then letting out a mighty sneeze,

she placed her head upon her knees

and listened to the noisy clock,

counting time, tick, tock, tick, tock.

Minutes passed but they seemed like hours

as Pati dreamed of fields and flowers,

wishing she could join her friends

and play games in the sun again.

A friendly mouse was passing by

and noticed Pati as she began to cry,

first with little gentle yowls

but growing into deep, sad growls.

"Oh, please come home" she seemed to say.

"All I want to do is play.

I hate being here all on my own,

it's the saddest time I've ever known".

The mouse looked on with a worried face.

He'd been rushing off to an important place

but seeing Pati crying there,

he knew he had to stop and care.

Because no matter what, it's true to say,

in this busy world we have today,

lending a hand to those in need

is about as important as things can be.

Now, fortunately, this particular mouse

was the smartest mouse in the entire house.

Perhaps the smartest in the entire street,

the smartest mouse you could ever hope to meet.

And he had an idea so big and neat

it almost knocked him off his feet.

He knew precisely what to do

to cheer up Pati in a moment or two.

And sneaking behind a nearby sheet,

he gripped a coat hanger with his feet

and another with his tiny hands,

then said in a loud voice, deep and grand,

"Hey there little dog, it's me,

a friendly ghost who's come to see

what it is that could be so bad

to make you feel so low and sad?"

And as these booming words were said

he raised the coat-hangers above his head

to make the sheet grow large and tall

as he wobbled towards Pati down the hall.

Now, at first, Pati got a massive a fright,

to see such a peculiar sight.

She'd seen many strange things in her dreams,

but this was the first ghost she'd ever seen.

But as the friendly ghost came near

she realised she need have no fear,

and that the ghost had come to be

her friend and keep her company.

And so Pati told the friendly ghost

just what had been upsetting her the most,

and why she'd been crying behind the door

curled up in a ball on the hallway floor.

And while the ghost listened with a friendly ear

he wiped away all of Pati's tears,

until before she knew it she was happy again,

chatting with her ghostly friend.

"You're never really alone you know"

said the ghost just as he turned to go,

"with kindness and love in your heart and head

there's magic everywhere you tread".

And as he spoke these loving words

Pati heard her brother and sisters return,

charging fast into the hall,

running about and having a ball.

"Hey there sis', how have you been?

We hope that you don't think we're mean

to have played out but left you home

stuck behind this door alone".

"But I wasn't alone..." Pati began to say,

as she turned to point the other way,

but saw nothing but an empty sheet

and two old coat-hangers at her feet.

THE END

Clever Rose

And The

Mucky Beach

The stick flew through the morning air

and Rose dashed after it without a care.

She couldn't think of a better way

to start a long, hot summer's day.

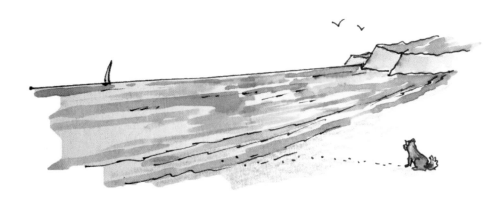

To chase and fetch upon the shore,

what happy dog could want for more?

with her loving human by her side,

throwing sticks into the foamy tide.

Rose was having so much fun,

running circles in the sun

and bringing back the sticks that flew

and floated in the ocean blue.

"Oh, how wonderful and grand

to leave my pawprints in the sand

and then watch the sea wash them away

to wipe the beach clean for another day".

But then, suddenly, she saw a sight

that gave Rose the most dreadful fright.

Beyond a great big washed up fish,

were piles and piles of smelly rubbish.

For a moment Rose just stood and stared.

How could it be that no-one cared

for such a special golden place?

To get so mucky seemed such a waste.

"Oh dear" said her human, with a shiver,

"It must be coming from the river.

The rubbish floats along the stream

and makes the nearby sea unclean".

"I'm sure that people just don't know

where their dropped litter's going to go.

They don't mean it, I'm sure that's true,

but whatever are we going to do?"

"To leave it here seems oh so bad,

but there's just so much, it makes me sad".

And Clever Rose could feel it too,

looking about, so much to do.

But then all of a sudden, she had an idea.

The answer to the mucky beach was clear.

It might be hard, that much was true,

but Rose knew what she had to do.

And letting out an excited bark,

she ran back to the beachside park

and rounded up her furry friends,

everyone with a paw to lend.

Her brother and her sisters came,

excited to play the cleaning game,

and so did Mac, the Scotty dog,

and his Chihuahua friend, Little Pog.

Alfred the Great Dane arrived,

with all his children by his side,

and dozens more from all around

came to check out the mighty sound.

Of dogs and owners in the sun,

picking up litter and having fun.

"Nice to see you, how do you do?

Isn't it wonderful what many hands can do!"

Together they worked, bringing back the gleam,

of a sparkling beach all nice and clean.

But Clever Rose worked hardest by far,

running around like a racing car.

One minute she was over there

collecting up a garden chair.

And moments later, back again,

picking up a chewed up pen.

Until, when she felt she could chase no more,

she stopped and gazed upon the shore

and looked upon the most wondrous sight

of a golden beach all bathed in light.

All around upon the sand

were happy owners shaking hands,

with tired dogs, ready for home,

cooling their paws in the soft white foam.

It really had been so much fun

to work together in the sun.

And here came her human, face aglow,

to say "Rose, you're the cleverest dog I know".

THE END

Lovely Leela Finds A Family

Thunder and lightning lit up the sky
as little lost Leela tried her best to stay dry.

Searching for a place where she could keep warm

and stay safe in such a frightening storm.

For days now she'd wandered, afraid and alone,

without any place that she could call home,

there had been family, but now they were gone,

and little lost Leela didn't know what she had done?

Had she been naughty? Had she been bad?

All she knew for sure was that now she was sad.

They'd left her by the roadside and got in the car,

now Leela was searching, walking ever so far.

Drinking from puddles and eating from bins,

Leela had already gotten so thin.

She could hardly remember her food bowl before,

had it even been real, she was no longer sure?

Crying a little as she curled in a ball,

above her the rain continued to fall.

As she tried to sleep in this wet and cold place,

then all of a sudden she saw a smiling face.

"Hello little dog, what are you doing here?

you're crying I see, don't shed any more tears.

Come home with me, I'll be your friend.

Let's see if we can't find your family again".

So Leela rested in safety that very same night,

waking the moment the day became light

to find the smiling face waiting for her

with food and a hot bath to clean all her fur.

For the next week she waited,

cared for in style,

but no family came,

it had been such a long while.

Until one day on the beach Leela looked up to find

some new people looking down with faces so kind.

"Oh my aren't you lovely" the new people said,

reaching out gently to stroke Leela's head,

wouldn't it be fantastic to have a friend just like you?

So pretty and happy, and so very cute.

Just a few short days later the new people returned

and said "hello Leela, you have a new home.

You're coming with us, we hope that's okay.

We're going to love you. What do you say?"

Though Leela was nervous, she stayed quiet and calm,

held safely and firmly in the new pair of arms,

as they carried her away to another new home.

Would this be forever? Leela still didn't know.

As the next days unfolded Leela looked on unsure,

who were these new people who'd opened their door?

Inviting her in and tending her needs,

from walking and playing to bath-time and feeds.

With a new, soft clean basket and a bowl on the floor,

the time flew by quickly, it was a week, maybe more

when Leela began to feel happy that she'd ended up here,

bringing an end to all her worries and fear.

THE END

THE REAL PUPPY PACK STORY

These joy filled stories have been inspired by incredible true events. In 2017, Dan and Esther crossed paths with a little ginger and white stray dog on the Southern Coast of Spain.

3 years earlier Dan had been rushed into emergency surgery and the couple were told to say "a proper goodbye, just in case". Dan did eventually recover and it kickstarted a search for a new way of life as the couple drove away from their lives in Durham in a second-hand campervan.

It was during their travels that they came across the little dog, who had been abandoned with no collar or chip, and who had been found sheltering during a huge storm by a lady called Blanca. There is a huge problem of dogs being abandoned in Spain, where dogs often get driven out to rural villages and left there.

Esther and Dan decided the campervan had room for one more. They named her Leela and instantly they became a very contented travelling trio. But bedraggled and very skinny little Leela was hiding a big surprise. Two weeks later, Bella, George, Rose, Pati, Teddy and Jess arrived! Dan and Esther committed to raising them and finding them good homes.

Whilst Teddy and Jess found their new homes with some amazing friends, for one reason or another, Bella, George, Pati and Rose stayed and joined the travelling team for the next 3 years. Both humans and all five dogs enjoyed incredible adventures as they travelled through Europe, mostly in the campervan but sometimes house-sitting.

From the beautiful sandy beaches of Spain, to chasing butterflies through sunflower fields in rural France, to riding cable cars up into the snowy mountains of Switzerland, they spread smiles (and a lot of woofs) wherever they went! Bella and Rose even took Esther for a very long, 27 day dog walk across the French Pyrenean mountains... But that's a whole other adventure story!

Dan wrote the first of these stories (Awesome George Saves The Day) as a gift for Esther when the pups were just a few months old and they were house-sitting in France. As the pups grew, it was wonderful to watch them play as a family but also watch their individual characters developing, which Dan captures in these stories.

During their travels Dan and Esther experienced so much kindness from complete strangers that it changed their whole worldview. From this kindness and also from the absolute love and joy the dogs radiated, Dan, a former scientific academic, drew inspiration and creativity.

It was always Esther's dream to one day see these stories being read to children but neither she nor Dan could draw. 3 years on and during the COVID19 lockdowns in April 2020, Esther, Dan and the dogs found themselves back at the same housesit where the pups had grown up. Determined to see her dream come true, Esther used the extra time to reach out for help.

It was the wonderfully kind and talented, retired PE teacher, Kim Prior who answered the call. Thanks to her beautiful illustrations it has been possible to bring these stories to life.

Our hope is that both children and adults enjoy and benefit from these stories. The cost has been kept as low as possible so that they have the potential to reach and make smile as many children as possible. Any small proceeds go to topping up the dogs "bone" accounts!

So thank you and woof woof for purchasing this book .....
Leela, Bella, Rose, Pati & George

You can read more about the dogs and see their individual profiles at:

http://www.estheranddan.com/p/meettheteam

You can read about Esther and Dan's full story in the book **"What Adventures Shall We Have Today?"**, in which Dan captures the very best travel tales from 6 years on the road. Naturally the dogs are the stars of half of this book, which is also available on Amazon.

Dan's inspiration also led to the creation of another collection of heart-warming and emotional dog poems, which combined with pictures, is a great gift for dog lovers of any age and guaranteed to bring joy, laughter and maybe even a tear or two.

"Love, Fluff and Chasing Butterflies" is also available on Amazon as an eBook and paperback and 50% of the royalties are donated to the Dogs Trust.

ALSO BY DAN, ESTHER & KIM

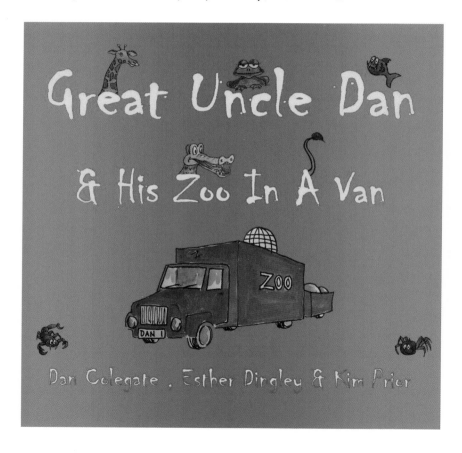

Great Uncle Dan

& His Zoo In A Van

ZOO

DAN 1

Dan Colegate . Esther Dingley & Kim Prior

Printed in Great Britain
by Amazon

51368428R00104